love your

QUEEN

SARDINE

*and
Princess
Persia*

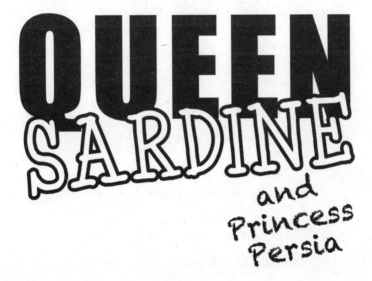

QUEEN SARDINE

and Princess Persia

Kate Willis-Crowley

templar

A TEMPLAR BOOK

First published in the UK in 2015 by Templar Publishing,
part of the Bonnier Publishing Group,
Northburgh House, 10 Northburgh Street, London EC1V 0AT

www.bonnierpublishing.com

Text and illustrations © Kate Willis-Crowley 2015

A CIP catalogue record for this book is available from the British Library.

ISBN: 978-1-84877-421-6

1 3 5 7 9 10 8 6 4 2

Printed and bound by Clays Ltd, St Ives Plc

For Phoebe

BACK TO SCHOOL

I'm Ivy. I'm eight years old, and my best friend is a cat. We've just had the greatest ever summer together, me and Queen Sardine, but now school's started again and I've had to leave her at home.

Good thing too, probably, because it's the very first day back and all the kids are going bonkersly bonkers! I've walked in with my mate Kei this morning.

Kei's always a bit hyper, but today she's close to bursting my eardrums! All because of this holiday-homework thingamajig we've been working on.

"Everyone's going to be talking about our dance!" she says, nudging me as we bundle into class. "They'll all be like, 'Oooh, there go Ivy 'n' Kei... let's get their autographs', like we're celebrities or something!"

She's totally exaggerating, and totally over the top, of course. But that's just Kei: happy and hectic and hilarious.

"All right, settle down!" hollers Mr Gubbins, but of course no one's listening.

Yeouch! A pencil sharpener just whacked me on the forehead!

"Sorry," giggles Jacob, "I was aiming for *him*!" He points at Marvin, and I duck as a pen lid pings out of Marvin's hand, straight into Jacob's nose.

"QUIET!" yells Mr Gubbins, and suddenly everyone *is* quiet, even Kei (and, believe me, it's nearly impossible to get her to stop chatting). But the thing is, Mr Gubbins isn't alone at the front of the class. There's a new girl with him, and everyone's listening to find out who she is.

"This is Marcy," he says, giving the girl an encouraging smile. "Marcy, would you like to introduce yourself?"

Marcy looks around the room, her blue eyes wide and worried, then shakes her head.

"No thanks, Mr Gubbins," she whispers. Marcy's cheeks are flushed a ruddy pink, and her ginger hair is pulled into a high ponytail. She's small. Maybe the smallest in our class, and I wonder how crazy-scary we must seem to this neat little new girl.

"Can I sit down?" she asks.

Poor Marcy...

"She can sit here, Mr G!" says Kei, pointing to the spare chair at our table.

"*Mr Gubbins*, thank you, Keilly," says Mr G, but he nods to Marcy and she scurries over to join us.

Kei immediately starts quizzing Marcy with whispered questions: *Where'd you move here from? Got brothers and sisters?*

Packed lunch or school dinners? That kind of thing. And it turns out Marcy *used* to live with her mum, in the city, but now she's living with her dad, in the old schoolhouse, which is basically right next to school. And then I notice everyone's looking at me, which can only mean one thing: Mr Gubbins just asked me something and I wasn't listening. Oops.

"Well, Ivy? Kei? Have you been practising for the class assembly? The talent show?"

Mr Gubbins came into our old class just before summer, and said we'd been lumped with doing the first class assembly after the holidays. First thing Monday morning, second week back… in front of the whole school. Gubbins seemed kind of grumpy about it. Anyway, he said we could do it like a talent show, so that we could prepare and practise our acts over the holidays. Me and Kei had this idea that we could do a dance…

"You two promised us a…" Mr Gubbins checks his list, "a dance with glitter sprinkles?" He sniffs at the 'glitter sprinkles' bit and I stifle a giggle.

I can't help

5G Assembly
INTRO
Poem = ?
* Poem = Esther
* Juggling - Mustafa & George
* play - Ella, Tye, Leila, Phoebe
* Dance (with glitter) - Ivy & Kei
* Puppet show - Rose & Jo

giggling. The glitter was Kei's idea.

"Yeah...Yup – I mean, yes, Mr Gubbins," I say. "We're almost ready now." Almost.

This is *almost* true. I mean we have practised. A bit.

A very little bit.

"Great, so you'll be ready to perform on Monday," he tells us. Then he catches sight of Marcy, and seems to pause in thought. "Yes..." he says to himself, drumming his pen on his list. "Marcy...Yes, Marcy, I'd like you to join Ivy and Kei's performance. Can't have you left out of the show, eh?" And, just like that, Marcy lights up, flashing a bright, white sunbeam smile.

"Oh thanks, Mr Gubbins!" she says. "I mean..." she looks from me to Kei, nibbling her bottom lip, "if it's okay with you two?"

I glance over at Kei and she shrugs. Well, that settles it. Looks like Marcy's going to be dancer number three.

"Brilliant!" she gushes. "Show me at break?"

"Uh... sure," I say, but the thing is, we

don't really *know* the dance properly yet. How are we going to teach it to Marcy without looking hopelessly hopeless?

There's no time to worry about that now. We've got maths: times tables, more stuff I was meant to practise over the holidays. And I kind of did. I'm not *totally* confused. Though Marcy seems to think I am. She keeps whispering the answers to me and Kei, and I know she's just trying to be helpful but it is a bit irritating, and – oh dear – Kei's starting to pout. Kei always pouts before she snaps, and poor Marcy doesn't see it coming...

$9 \times 5 = 45$

$5 \times 7 = 35$

$8 \times 7 = 56$

$4 \times 6 = 24$

$3 \times 7 = 21$

"I can do it myself!" Kei blurts out, making Marcy gasp.

Oh Christmas...

"Sorry, sorry – I didn't mean..." stumbles Kei, frowning. "I just, I..."

TRRRINNNGGG-ALING-ALING!

The bell rings for breaktime and I decide to change the subject.

"Come on, we'll show you round the playground."

Marcy half smiles, nods, and links her arm in mine. She pulls us together, with Kei tagging alongside looking kind of left out, but hey... Marcy's new. Kei will understand!

At least, that's what I thought at half-past ten. By the time the home bell rings I'm not so sure.

Today, Marcy has:

1. Watched us do our dance in the playground, shaking her head the *whole* way through.

2. Tried to add this impossible twirly jump to the dance. I was worse than useless, and Kei... Kei tried *so* hard but *still*

ended up on her bum, huffy and covered in grass stains.

3. Told us we should leave out the glitter sprinkles. Madness! The glitter sprinkles are the best bit! Without glitter sprinkles, it'll just be us, prancing about like idiots, falling on our backsides in front of *everyone ever.*

The sprinkles are staying!

So yeah, I was wrong – Kei's not feeling *understanding* at all. Her normally-mega-watt smile is a stiff straight line.

This cannot be good.

But hey, they're both coming back to mine after school today so we can go through the dance again. So there's plenty of time for them to start getting along better. Or possibly – very possibly – plenty of time for things to get ugly.

UGLY

Did I mention that Kei is my neighbour's granddaughter? Granny Mo lives in the flat above me and Mum, and she's got soooo many grandkids that even I call her Granny. So whenever Kei wants to come over to play it's easy peas because

she can stay over at Granny Mo's and go to school with me the next day. It's brilliant.

Kei and I walk dead fast and we're almost home now, but Marcy has nipped back to hers to check if she's allowed round mine for tea and practice. Is it bad of me that I'm hoping her dad'll say 'no'? Urgh, I hate thinking something so mean but I've got a bad feeling in my tummy over this. I'm all queasy with worry, trying to keep both Kei and Marcy happy, when it just feels impossible!

When we get home, Queen Sardine is waiting for me on the front step! I tickle her forehead while Kei quickly nips upstairs to say hi to Granny Mo.

Now, cos Sardine is my absolute best friend ever, I tell her all about Marcy straight away, thinking (hoping) she'll understand why I'm getting in a tizzy.

She doesn't.

"Really, Ivy, I'm sure it's not that bad. Now how's about fetching me a little cream, there's a dear…"

Ha. That's what you get when your bestie's a talking cat! I take her inside and close the door behind us.

"I mean it, Your Majesty! She gets all bossy, like she knows *everything* about *everything*, and Kei's going to lose her temper if she's not careful!"

Sardine's not really paying attention. She biffs a dust bunny as she trots down the hall in front of me. "Yes, well, you humans do get like that sometimes. Now, about my cream . . ."

Honestly! I sigh, reaching the kitchen with its big magnet-covered fridge, then fetch her a saucer of cream.

"It's bad for you, that stuff," I mumble, but she's too busy lapping to care.

I hear Kei skipping up the hall just as Mum comes in from the bathroom.

"Hi, Kei! Hi, angel!" She must've been cleaning because she's wearing pink rubber gloves, and smells bleachy. Maybe I should've phoned home to ask her about Marcy coming over... Oops.

DING DONG!

Here goes... "Er, Mum, is it okay if our friend Marcy comes over too?"

DING DONG! DING DONG!

"Geez, Marcy," grumbles Kei, "give us a sec..."

Mum raises her eyebrows at Kei then looks at me. "Marcy... I don't know a Marcy, do I? Well, come on, better let the poor girl in, eh?" she says. So we do.

Marcy's dad is outside in a slick, shiny red car, leaning out of a rolled-down window.

"Greetings, madam!" he shouts to Mum. "Awfully good of you to have my Marcy. Seven o'clock pick-up suit you?"

Mum is about to say 'yes', I think, but it doesn't matter, because Marcy's dad doesn't wait for an answer. He revs the engine, saluting out of the window. "Later, folks!" he calls, already pulling away from the curb, and then he's off.

"Hi, Marcy," Mum says, and Marcy looks at her feet, shuffly and shy again.

It's weird. When we're doing the dance

stuff she's like a different person. All brave and pushy. But now...

"Hi, Mrs... Ivy's mum," she whispers.

I grab her hand and pull her down the hall to the kitchen, and soon we're pushing the table to one side to give us room to dance.

I move Sardine's saucer into a corner and she pads up beside me. "Well, Marcy seems nice enough. Honestly, Ivy, you can be so sensitive," she whispers.

"Oooh! You've got a cat?" says Marcy, getting braver now that she's stretching, warming up ready to dance. "How sweet. I've always wanted a cat."

Queen Sardine beams, giving me a look that says, "*See?*"

But Marcy hasn't finished. "Though, I'd like one of those really *pretty* cats, you know? A pedigree. Like that super-cute Persian I saw at the end of your road."

Oh… my… The expression on Queen Sardine's face seems to be stuck somewhere between horrified and distraught.

"A *'pretty'* cat! And what am I, then? Little Miss Ugly Whiskers?" she hisses. "And – and – and *what* Persian down the road? The girl's nuts!"

I look Marcy over, really look at her, to see if she can understand what Sardine's saying, like me. I've only met one other person who can, but you never know. Marcy doesn't look like she understands, though.

I dip down to stroke Her Majesty's head. "You *are* pretty, Queen Sardine," I try to reassure her.

"Queen Sardine! Oh, yes, I love that! So clever!" laughs Marcy.

"Clever?" asks Kei, and I really wish she hadn't.

Queen Sardine's tail swishes as she stares at Marcy. Perhaps I should put Her Majesty politely outside. Maybe with some extra cream!

"Well, yes! It's funny because she looks so normal, you know. So unlike a queen. I mean, she's lovely, of course... Oh dear - you know what I mean, don't you?" She looks from me to Kei, her face reddening, but it's not us she's offended.

Queen Sardine vibrates with a low rumbling growl, and this time, when she speaks, I can barely understand her.

Hiss... normal?// hiss... how... hiss... dare she?/ ...hiss!

"Are you sure she's tame?" asks Marcy.

Before Queen Sardine has a chance to swipe Marcy with her claws, I pull her into my arms and carry her outside.

"It's *her* you should be putting out!" Sardine snaps. " *'Tame'*?"

"Your Majesty, I don't think Marcy meant to be rude... And of course you're not *normal*." Oops, that came out wrong. "I mean you're much *more than* normal. You're... extra-normal... super-normal..."

What's wrong with me? When did words become so dangerously tricky? I manage to stop talking before I say something even stupider, and I ask Sardine to wait on the doorstep while I fetch a few feel-better treats from the kitchen.

Eventually I leave my furry friend with cream and fish and a sprinkling of cat biscuits, and a big, big 'sorry'.

I know Marcy didn't *mean* to be rude – and of course she has no idea that Her Majesty could have understood what she said and taken offence but I can't help feeling a teensy bit cross with her for upsetting my best friend.

When I get back to the girls, I can see it's going to be a loooooong evening. Mum seems to be hiding somewhere, and I wish I could do the same. Because Marcy's being a bossy dance expert again. She's telling Kei to 'watch her posture', whatever that means. And she's tutting each time Kei does a spin.

Marcy thinks she's making all our moves better but really she's making them *harder*, and me and Kei, we just can't seem to *do* what she wants us to! But Marcy doesn't seem to notice Kei's tooth-grinding, nostril-flaring, slow-burning rage.

"We know most of it," I say, trying to finish up before Kei flips. "Maybe we can just make the rest up as we go along?"

"Good grief, no. Look, I know you both need a lot of practice. I mean, like, loads! But you've got me to help you. Shall we go from the top?"

So we start again. Over and over,

practising, practising, 'watching our postures'. And the whole time I'm terrified Kei's going to explode.

Seriously, Kei's about to blow, any minute now. She's crossed her arms all tense and tight, and she's jutting out her chin, and I can feel the *'KABOOM!'* coming in 5, 4, 3, 2, 1...

But just as she finally screams "Stop!", Mum enters the kitchen to make dinner.

"Stop?" I ask Kei., trying to avoid disaster. "Oh, yes, stop... We've got to stop so Mum can cook. Good thinking."

STOP!

Kei glares at me, then sighs. She knows I'm trying to keep everyone friendly, and though she's

not happy about it, she plays along. "Yeah, better stop for now," she mumbles, and Marcy smiles and shrugs, oblivious to the throttling I just saved her from.

I could dance for joy when seven o'clock comes around, and Marcy's dad arrives to take her home.

Waving goodbye, as that flashy red car hurtles down the road, Kei turns to face me. "What are we going to do?" she says. "She's making it impossible!"

But there's nothing we *can* do, is there?

Whenever we tell Marcy that her routine is too hard, she says we need more practice, and it's not like we can boot her out of the performance. Mr G would be furious!

Queen Sardine mews at my ankle, and I pull her into my arms.

"Don't worry," I tell her. "Marcy's gone, and she didn't mean to upset you."

"Oh, Ivy, you silly thing, I'm not worried about *her*," Sardine says. "No, it's that cat I'm worried about. That *pedigree*! I've heard things, Ivy. *Bad* things!"

Sardine really does look flustered. She goes on, "While you were playing ballerina, I was playing detective, and do you know what I found out?"

"Go on," I say.

"Well," she continues, "her name is *Princess Persia*." Queen Sardine grimaces as she says the name, like she's just smelled something icky. "And it turns out that *everyone* – all the Kipper Street cats – they *all* think she's… she's…"

Queen Sardine looks away and takes a deep breath.

"What?" I say. "What is she? Mean? Dangerous? What?"

"*Adorable!*" she snarls.

And there it is.

Oh crumbs.

Her Majesty is jealous.

CATTITUDE

The next morning, I get maybe halfway down the road when Sardine catches up with me.

She pads at my heels, an angry glint in her eye, and I have absolutely no clue what she's up to.

"You're up to something," I tell her.

Her Majesty's tail is twitching as she walks, so I know she's agitated.

"Whatever gives you that idea?" she asks. "You're being... odd."

She flutters her eyelashes, acting all innocent. "Odd?" she says. "What's odd about two best friends taking a walk?"

Uh-huh... *That's* what this is. Just two friends taking a walk. Sure. Nothing to do with the large, blue Persian cat I can see as we near the end of the road. Of course not.

I stop dead, but Queen Sardine just marches straight on.

There's no stopping her.

"Wait," I say, "if you're only here to hassle that new cat, then—"

"Look!" hisses Sardine. "Look, there she is! Stretched out on that windowsill like she owns the street... How dare she?"

Princess Persia is soaking up the morning sun, her beautiful silky-soft fur rippling in the breeze. Wailing opera music pours through the open window of her people's house, and she looks... blissful.

That is, until Queen Sardine comes along.

"Ahem," coughs Sardine, trying to get the other cat's attention.

The big bow on
her head rises and
falls as she breathes,
but the cat doesn't move. She doesn't
even flinch.

"I don't think she heard you. Let's just
go!" I whisper.

"Ahem!" This time Her Majesty
shouts it.

The Persian opens one sleepy eye.

"Yes?" she yawns.

As she raises her head, I'm almost

blinded by her dazzling, jewelled collar.

Queen Sardine tuts. "I suppose you don't know who I am. I'm your queen. You may call me Your Majesty," she says, jutting her chin into the air.

"Well," drawls the Persian, "if you don't mind, *Your Majesty*, I'm sleeping…"

Her eyes droop closed again.

"Sleeping!" yowls Her Royal Stressy-ness.

Persia opens her eyes again, frowning and confused. "Erm… yes?"

"When royalty addresses one, one bows or curtsies. One does not sleep!"

Good grief. Sardine's being a total nightmare!

"One sleeps when one wants to sleep," says Persia through gritted teeth, though she doesn't sound sleepy any more. In fact, Princess Persia sounds cross. Dangerously cross.

"Cheek of it!" she says in a whispered hiss. (Sardine does it so often, I've given it a name: *the hiss-per.*) "Thinks she can act all la-dee-dah, eh?"

"If you don't mind, I'd like some privacy," says Persia. She gives one silky paw a long lick, and wipes it daintily against her head. Then she closes her eyes and sways in time to the music. "I do like a bit of opera in the morning, don't you? Best enjoyed *alone*, though, if you catch my drift?"

"Yes, maybe we should come back later," I suggest to my clearly-crazy best friend, but she totally ignores me.

Queen Sardine narrows her eyes, and licks one of *her* paws.

"Thinks she's grander than me, does

she?" she hiss-pers. "I'll show her grand!"

Queen Sardine springs onto the window sill, coming nose to nose with the shocked Persian, who bristles and flattens her ears.

"What do you think you're doing?" she says.

"I am your queen!" Sardine growls, and I think she's about to swing at the other cat. Her paw lifts high into the air, claws out, and then, just as I'm about to yell 'stop'... she *does* stop. Something's got her attention. Or, I should say, some*one*.

"Morning, Your Majesty," says Benny. He bounds into the garden, coming to a stop beneath where they're squabbling. "Who's your friend?"

As always when Benny's about, Queen Sardine gets all weird and girly and shy... "Oh, who – this?" she says, quickly pulling back her claws and backing away from the Persian.

"Princess Persia, isn't it? I been 'earing about you, Miss. Pleased to meet you. Benny's the name. Sir Benny, in fact."

Persia looks at Sardine, then at Benny, like she's working something out. Then she hops down, rubs her head against Benny's, and tells him she's 'charmed' to meet him! *Charmed!*

Oh dear... Queen Sardine won't like that one bit (and I guess that's the point!) Benny is Sardine's almost-boyfriend, or – I don't know – whatever the cat version of boyfriend is.

"Yeah, nice to meet you too, Miss," he says, but he's not really looking at Persia. Like always, he's only got eyes for Queen Sardine.

"You didn't tell me we had such a

handsome chap in the neighbourhood," Princess Persia teases.

Queen Sardine only seems able to growl – deep and low, like a miniature tiger.

Benny looks concerned. "You all right, Ma'am?"

Sardine says nothing, just glares a *don't-mess-with-me* glare in Persia's direction.

"She does look a little *odd*, doesn't she?" Persia says with a mean chuckle. But Benny doesn't notice.

As much as I want to help out my furry friend, I really haven't got time for this.

"Your Majesty," I whisper. "I'm going to be late for school."

Sardine looks at me and manages to stop growling.

"Fine," she mutters through gritted teeth. "I'm done here. Let's go."

"Leaving so soon?" asks Princess Persia, cosying up to Benny. What he *doesn't* see is Persia then turning to Queen Sardine and mouthing, "Good!"

"Allow me to walk you home, Ma'am, 'specially if you're feelin' peaky," Benny offers, but before Sardine can reply, Persia speaks up.

"Oh, yes, *do* let us take you home, Your Majesty," she trills in a sugary little voice.

And by now Sardine's too cross for words. All she can do is shake her head and flounce off, over the garden fence.

"Something I said?" purrs Princess Persia.

I roll my eyes. They're as bad as each

other, Princess Persia and Queen Sardine. And I really don't want to be getting in the middle of their tiff!

"See you later, Benny," I say, bending to stroke his raggedy fur. "Nice to meet you," I mumble at the princess.

She raises a stroppy eyebrow at me, as if to say '*Was* it?' then turns her back on me, purring and smiling at Sir Benny.

Hmph! So it looks like I've been given the cold-kitty-shoulder from the new cat on the block.

Well, whatever.

I'm not going to waste time worrying about her bad attitude. Not when I've got my own new-girl problem to deal with.

SPLAT!

Whew! I get to school just as the bell rings, and there, by the gate, are Marcy and Kei. Marcy's all smiles and chatter, but Kei looks miffed.

"You're late," says Marcy, smiling. "Come on!" And she leads the way inside.

Kei lags behind. "Yeah, Ivy, you're late," she grumbles, her voice all hushed. "Which means I've had to listen to her

gushing on and on about our stupid dance routine, all on my own! I swear, the girl's obsessed!"

"She's not that bad," I say, but Kei doesn't look convinced.

"Oooooh, goody! Looky look!" calls Marcy as we reach the classroom. She points at the whiteboard, where Mr Gubbins has displayed today's timetable.

Urgh, I don't believe it! Looks like we'll be rehearsing for the talent show *all afternoon*. Which means trying to keep Kei from yelling at Marcy. More squabbling over glitter sprinkles. And, most likely, lots of falling on our bums and looking like idiots.

Except, in the end, that's not what happens. This is what happens. And it's bad. It's VERY bad.

We slog through a dull morning of maths. We play whole-class tag all breaktime. Then it's

English. Then it's lunchtime, and we've been getting on pretty well, chatting about loads of stuff, but not dancing. And yeah, Kei's huffed a couple of times – like when Marcy paired up with me in the dinner line, Kei hated that – but mostly it's all been fine. Then...

Okay, so I'm just in the middle of putting away my tray when Kei sneaks up behind me, and says right into my ear, "Looky look!" in a perfect Marcy voice.

I gasp and leap

about a mile in the air. It's a miracle that I don't drop my tray. Though a little bit of leftover mash does manage to leap off my plate, splatting onto the 'KEEP YOUR SCHOOL TIDY' sign, and a teeny blob of mushy peas flips through the air, into Kei's hair.

With a finger, she touches her head, locates the green goo and holds a blob out for me to see. Then she says it again, "Looky look!"

When Kei sticks her finger in her mouth and goes *'Mm-mmmmmm'* like my cold mushy peas are the best thing she's ever tasted, I get almighty, shoulder-shaking giggles. And Kei keeps on going...

"You're late! Come on, girlies: practise, practise! Show me those pointy toes!"

She's making stuff up now, but Kei's voice is an exact copy of Marcy's, and I'm laughing so hard tears are streaking my cheeks. After all this stressing over Marcy and the dance it feels good to giggle again, just me and Kei.

But Kei doesn't seem to notice that she's getting louder, and I can't catch my breath to tell her... She keeps repeating, "Ivy Meadows, you're a messy mess, but lucky for you I'm here to help! Me! Marvellous Marcy, dancer extraordinaire!"

And that's when Marcy appears.

My eyes are still blurry from laughing, but when I hear her voice, suddenly nothing's funny at all.

"I hate you!" Marcy cries, thrusting her tray, clanging and clattering, onto the trolley. Then she dashes full speed out of the hall, with the dinner ladies yelling after her to 'STOP RUNNING, NOW!'

But Marcy doesn't stop.

What have we done?

For a moment neither Kei or I move.

The mashed potato goo slops down from the poster, splashing onto the floor.

"We should probably leave her to calm down," I whisper.

"Yeah," says Kei, "she wouldn't want us to follow. Best leave her alone for a bit..."

So instead of running after Marcy, like we know we really ought to, Kei and I skulk outside into the raucous playground, and huddle underneath the climbing frame.

"She did *kind of* deserve it, didn't she?"

Kei looks at me, and before I can even answer she covers her face with her hands. "No, I know... Don't say it."

"It wasn't only you," I say, and it's true. I kind of wish it had been just Kei, and I didn't feel so guilty, but no. I was laughing too. Laughing at Marcy. Thinking it didn't matter because she couldn't see it happening. But even if she hadn't shown up out of nowhere, it still would've mattered. It would've and it *does*.

So there's only one thing for it. It's time to say sorry. Which should be easy, right?

WRONG

Knowing you've done something wrong, and upset someone, is the worst feeling ever.

When the bell rings, Marcy stands at the back of the line and trails into our classroom really slowly as we shuffle back to our desks. I try to catch her eye but she won't look at me. She sits at the other side of the table, head down, looking miserable.

"Er, Marcy," I begin, but she still doesn't look up.

"We're sorry," says Kei. "Really. We're really sorry." But Marcy doesn't respond, and then Mr Gubbins gives us his one-raised-eyebrow look, which means 'stop talking', so we do.

After taking the afternoon register Mr Gubbins gets the class to move all the chairs and tables out of the way, and we pretend the front of our classroom is the little stage in the school hall.

Josh mumbles an introduction.

"Welcome to Yellow Class's assembly. We have lots of hobbies... 'n' stuff... So we've decided to do a talent show so you can see what... see what – I've forgotten it, Mr G."

"So you can see what we do in our spare time. Learn it, Josh!"

Then we take it in turns rehearsing our performances. Everyone's practised something: Esther reads a poem about turkeys at Christmas, George and Mustafa do a juggling routine – accidentally

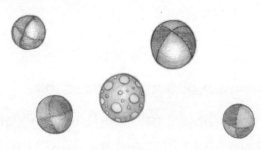

biffing Mr Gubbins on the head with a ball – Ella, Phoebe, Tye and Leila do a spooky play about headless ghouls and slime sandwiches, and then it's our turn. *Oh crackers.*

We move into our starting positions, me and Kei. Marcy doesn't move.

"Marcy!" whispers Kei.

Nothing.

"Marcy!" I whisper, but she ignores me and instead she raises her hand in the air, looking at Mr Gubbins.

"Er, yes, Marcy?"

"Mr Gubbins, sir. I don't feel too good," she says. She tells him she's got a tummy ache, and feels really sick, so he sends

her to go and see Mrs Singh in the main office. And that's the last we see of Marcy for the afternoon; she doesn't come back.

Kei and me, we do our dance, but our hearts aren't in it. Our spins are clumsy, our moves are jumbled and I can't help thinking maybe if we'd listened a bit harder to Marcy's advice, we might've been less of a disaster.

Everyone claps a bit too slowly, and we scurry back to the carpet feeling smaller and more embarrassed than ever.

"Marcy would've remembered those tricky bits, no problem," sighs Kei when the hometime bell finally rings.

"Yeah," I say. "I mean, she was bossy, but I don't think she meant to be. And without her we're . . ."

"We're rubbish," mumbles Kei.

I nod. Yeah. Rubbish.

As I pick up my bag I spot Marcy's rucksack on the floor by her chair. She must have forgotten it, and it's been knocked about by everyone grabbing and jostling to get their own stuff. There are pens and scraps of paper loose on the floor. I grab them, and I'm about to stick them back in Marcy's rucksack when—

"Oh!" says Kei. "Wait. What's that?" She pulls a photograph from my hands, I hadn't noticed it among the big A4 sheets. We both stare at the picture. It's of Marcy, standing next to a smiling woman who looks just like her but grown-up. Marcy's mum, I guess. Must be. Marcy's dressed up like a proper ballerina. Tutu and shiny slippers and *everything*. And she's holding the biggest trophy I've ever seen.

"Oh. Wow," stammers Kei.

Yeah. Wow. This is very... wow. Very wow indeed. Marcy is a proper

dancer, and we never knew. She didn't say!

We finish tidying up Marcy's stuff and hang her bag back on her peg.

"No wonder she got all excited over the dance…" Kei sighs, then hangs her head, looking exactly how I feel. Guilty, guilty, guilty.

Still, tomorrow we can sort it out. We'll say sorry to Marcy. A big, mahoosive sorry. She'll see how bad we're feeling, and we'll all be friends again. Simple.

Next morning I get to school crazy-early to talk to Marcy before the bell rings. Kei's done the same thing, and we wait nervously by the gate while all the other kids stream into the playground.

But Marcy doesn't show up.

She's not there the next

Tues

SEPTEMBER
Mon 9 | Tues 10
Wed " | Thurs 12
Fri 13 | Sat 14
Sun 15

Friday

day either, or the one after that.

And when she doesn't show up on Friday, I start to think that's it, no more Marcy. *All because of us.*

I can tell Kei is worried too. Her shoulders are slumped, and in class she's too distracted to work. She just chews her pen lid, frowning and doodling on the table. Like me, her mind's on one thing: Marcy.

At lunchtime we do the only thing we can think of. We write Marcy a letter.

Dear Marcy,

We miss you and we are really super-dooper sorry. It's the sorriest we've ever been, ever. You're new at Squiddly School, and it's probably really scary, and we should've been making you feel extra-welcome, not making jokes behind your back.

You ARE a brilliant dancer and we should have listened to your ideas. Please come back to school and be our friend again.

From Ivy and Kei

PS We've dumped the glitter sprinkles.

PPS Sorry, sorry, sorry, sorry and on and on forever!

After school I creep down the old school house drive and post the letter through the door, and I hope. I hope Marcy will read it. And I hope she'll forgive us. All I can do is hope.

THE MIDNIGHT LIE

It's late. I'm in bed, finally drifting off to sleep, when...

"Meeeowww! She said *what*, Your Majesty?" Benny's voice carries right through my bedroom window.

I sit upright and listen. My curtains are drawn, but a streetlamp shines in from outside and I can see the silhouettes of two cats, moving about on the window ledge.

"She said she's too good for Kipper Street. She said the Kipper Street cats are riff-raff – you especially!" says Queen Sardine.

Wow, this Princess Persia really *is* getting too big for her furry boots! Unless... No! Queen Sardine couldn't be making this up, could she? She wouldn't, would she?

"Well, that's no good. No good at all!" huffs Benny. "I'm tellin' the others. The Kipper Street cats need to know we've an enemy among us! 'Night, Your Majesty!"

"Good night, Sir Benny," she calls. Then – too late – Sardine seems to grasp what Benny's just said. "Hang on, 'enemy'? No, I just meant... Wait!" she yells, but Benny's silhouette has already disappeared. Sardine sighs. "She's not an *enemy* exactly," she continues softly, and that's when I hear the guilt in her voice. That's when I *know* she's made it all up.

Oh no. No, no, no, Queen Sardine... What have you done?

Poor Princess Persia!

I lie still, listening for the clip-clap sound of the catflap. Sure enough –

CLIP-CLAP!

– here comes Queen Sardine.

She slinks into my room, her shoulders sagging.

"Want to talk, Your Majesty?" I ask, knowing she must feel horrible.

"No, no," she says, plopping down onto the end of my bed, her head low.

"I overheard what you said to Benny," I tell her. "Princess Persia didn't *really* say that about the Kipper Street cats being riff-raff, did she?"

Queen Sardine snorts. "She's ever so lah-di-dah, you know... *Obviously* thinks she's better than the rest of us."

Hmm, she's avoiding the question. "But did she *say* it?" I repeat.

"She thinks it."

"That's not the same thing, and you know it!"

"So you're taking her side. Thanks a lot,"

Sardine mumbles, before turning her back on me.

She snuggles up to my favourite cuddly toy ever, Felina, with a grumpy 'hmph'.

"I'm not taking her side," I say. "You know I'm not. But if Benny and the others start picking on Persia, all because you lied . . ."

"I don't want to talk about it," she says, and starts gnawing at Felina's ears.

Fine, I think. *Be like that.*

I roll over and close my eyes, determined to fall asleep.

And, again, I'm just dozing off when I'm startled awake by angry yowls and meows from the street outside.

"What's going on?" we both yelp at once, springing up.

It sounds like every cat in the neighbourhood is out tonight, and... oh no!

"Down with Princess Persia!"

"Out! Out! Out!"

"Kipper Street doesn't want you!"

I drag myself out of bed and pull back the curtains. This is madness: there are cats everywhere. Hissing, mewling, growling cats. Cats prowling up the street towards Princess Persia's house...

What are they thinking? Do they think they can order her to leave Kipper Street?

"Princess Persia, we order you to leave!" yells one of them. It sounds like Benny. So, that's *exactly* what they're thinking.

Meanwhile, Queen Sardine's lying on my duvet, her paws covering her ears. She's wincing, like she can't quite bear to hear what's happening. Well, she has to hear it, and she has to fix it!

"You need to stop them!" I hiss-per (yes, I'm hiss-pering too now). "Stop them before they wake up the whole neighbourhood! Before they hurt Persia!"

Sardine sits up, whimpers, and says, "I know – I know I have to sort this out! But how can I? If I tell Benny I lied…"

I do feel sorry for my friend, I do, but…

"You have to do something, Your Majesty."

She looks me in the eye and nods. Then, head drooped low, she skulks from the room.

CLIP-CLAP!

– out she goes. And seconds later I see her shadow hurrying down the street.

"Halt!" she shouts. "Leave her! She's not worth your time."

"But, Your Majesty, she has to go! If the Kipper Street cats aren't good enough for her, she should leave," they howl.

I wish Sardine would tell them the truth and apologise for lying. I mean, I know saying sorry's not easy. I *know*, don't I? But if I can try surely she can too!

"I order you all to go home!" she calls. "Go on. Off you go, back to your people. We'll talk about her in the morning."

Along Kipper Street, lights are being flicked on. People are pulling back curtains and fiddling with blinds, probably wondering what on earth the cats are playing at.

MEOWL MEEEOOOW MEW
MEW MEWL

But with a few grumpy mewls and meows, the cats scatter back to their houses, and eventually I hear that

CLIP-CLAP!

sound again, just before Queen Sardine returns to my side.

"Happy now?" she huffs.

All I can do is stare at her in disbelief.

I'm too tired to argue, so I climb back into bed and pull my duvet up high.

I wait for Sardine to jump on the bed, but she doesn't.

In the end I roll onto my side, turning my back on my stroppy friend.

How can my best friend ask if I'm happy? I've upset Marcy, who won't believe I'm sorry, and Queen Sardine has upset all of the cats on Kipper Street and is too *proud* to say sorry. And

of the night, and I'm tired

So, no, I'm not happy.

Not happy at all.

MISSING

On Saturday morning I wake up late. Queen Sardine's gone, and I can't find Mum anywhere in the flat. Well, this is odd. Maybe she's outside?

I pull on my dressing gown and peer out of the front door, and – yup – there's Mum, scratching her head, and looking totally flummoxed. I can se why: there are cats dotted about the garden. Lots of cats. All the cats from Kipper Street. And they're sitting very calmly, facing towards the doorway like they're waiting for something.

"I– I heard them mewling," says Mum. "So I came outside to see if they were

hungry. But they're not. What do you think they want?"

I know exactly what they want. They want their queen.

"Where is she?" squeaks little Sprout, the smallest and youngest of all. "Where's Queen Sardine?"

Good question. Could she be with Princess Persia? Somehow I doubt it. She didn't seem keen to say 'sorry' last night, and I doubt that's changed.

I crouch down to talk to Sprout, glancing quickly over at Mum. Mum doesn't really understand this *talking to cats* business – she thinks it's just me playing games – so I try not to make it overly obvious. But she's not looking at me right now, thank goodness.

"She's not inside," I whisper. "Have you checked Cuttle Street? How about Crab Alley?" She has to be around here somewhere.

"No one's seen 'er," says Sprout. "Sausage 'n' Whiskers looked all over."

What does this mean? Is she lost? My

tummy flip-flops. Has Queen Sardine run away?

"Mum," I ask, "have you seen Queen Sardine?"

"Not since yesterday. Do you think that's why they're here? Do you think they're looking for her? No, that's bonkers," she says, shaking her head.

"Maybe," I reply, sighing. But I know they're looking for Her Majesty. "Mum? Can I play outside for a bit?"

She agrees, so I hurry indoors, pull on jeans and a long-sleeve t-shirt, then dash out on to Kipper Street. Queen Sardine can't have gone far.

All the Kipper Street cats join the search. Whiskers looks round the bins in Crab Alley. Sausage and Smudge sniff out Cuttle Street. The rest of the gang, including me, go up and down Kipper Street, peering into gardens, under cars and up trees, until we're sick with worry and totally exhausted.

"Ah, this ain't good," says Benny. "You know what I think, eh?"

I shake my head.

"I think Princess Persia's done somethin' with 'er Majesty. Eh? We'll 'ave to go confront 'er. What d'you say, cats? Who's with me?"

The cats hiss and spit in agreement.

"She must have Her Royal Highness trapped somewhere," hisses Molly.

"Only one way to find out," says Benny. "Let's go and find Princess Persia!"

"Wait! You can't just accuse her! It's not fair," I say. The cats all turn and look at me like I'm crazy.

"What would you 'ave us do then, Miss Ivy?" asks Benny.

Oh help! I have to say something.

"No, please!" I beg. "*I'll* go and see Persia. You keep on searching… look further than Kipper Street. We can't just go round accusing people."

"Hmph! If you say so, Miss, but I hope you're right. Cos if Persia's got 'er Majesty captive an' we're wastin' precious time…"

"If she has, I'll find out, won't I?" I say firmly, trying to reassure him. But honestly! Of course Persia's not holding Queen Sardine captive. Even if the

Princess *was* some kind of grizzly villain how on earth would she catnap a stonking great tabby? It would be like me trying to carry Kei!

When I get to Persia's house she's nowhere to be seen. Grey clouds are gathering above and the breeze peppers my skin with goosebumps.

Who wants to know?

"Princess!" I hiss-per. "Where are you?"

"Who wants to know?" quivers a frightened voice. It's coming from underneath a bush.

"Princess Persia? Is that you down there? It's Ivy, Queen Sardine's friend. I need to talk with you," I tell her. Very, slowly she slinks out of the undergrowth.

"What were you doing down there?"

Her eyes dart from side to side before she answers. "I've got to stay hidden. They're after me."

She turns her nose up. "So," she continues, "I suppose you've come to hassle me too? Honestly, that royal friend

of yours has to be the bossiest, pushiest, meanest cat I've ever met. She's been spreading rumours about me!"

"I know, she went too far," I admit. "But you're as bad as each other! Why did you have to get all lovey-dovey around Benny? You really upset her!

And I know she's sorry, but she's too proud to say it just yet, and... well, she's gone! She's disappeared, and I don't know what to do."

"Gone?" gasps Persia. "She can't be gone. She has to tell these loopy cats I didn't say those horrible things! It's not like the lovey-dovey stuff was really *real*. Heavens no! I just wanted... I wanted to get back at her."

"Well, it worked. And now you're both miserable." I sigh.

As I turn to go, she calls out.

"Listen," she says, "I hope your friend turns up. When she does, can you tell her what I just told you? Tell her she's got the wrong idea – I don't want to take Sir Benny away from her. I want to settle into Kipper Street without any fuss."

"I'll tell her," I promise. With that she nods, turns tail, and pads off round the side of her people's house, leaving me to look for my best friend.

Oh, Your Majesty, where are you? Did you run away? I need to know you're not still cross with me. I need to know you're safe – that you didn't flounce off and get lost or hurt. Queen Sardine, will you please, please, *please* come home!

WET WHISKERS

It's getting dark on Kipper Street. The dull, spongy clouds are getting thicker. Gloomier.

I'd better head back. Any minute now it's going to . . .

Rain.

Too late. The drops crash down, fast and heavy.

Well, that's just perfect. Queen Sardine's nowhere to be found, and I'm freezing, wet and miserable.

I trudge down the street, head down, not watching where I'm going, and when I go to cross the road... HONK! A bright red car breaks in front of me.

I jump in shock, trip up, and fall in the gutter. My heart hammers.

"Ivy! Are you all right?" It's Marcy's dad, and there's Marcy too, both of them climbing out to help me up.

"Sorry," I sniff, on the verge of tears. "Why... *sniff*... Why are you... *sniff*... here?"

"We found your cat!" says Marcy, pulling her coat off and holding it over both our heads.

Her dad pulls a big cardboard box from the back seat of the car. It's got air holes cut in the top, and I can hear something scrabbling to get out.

"Meeeeeow! Let me out NOW!"

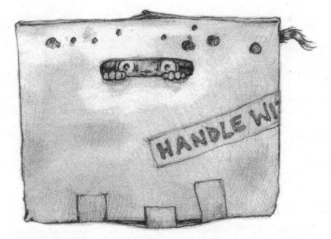

Queen Sardine!

Then I do cry, I can't help it. But it's a good kind of crying. A happy kind.

"You found her! Where was she?"

I open the box and Sardine scrambles out and into my arms. We're both getting wet but I couldn't care less. I study her face to check she's okay, and she winks at me! Hang on, what's she playing at?

"I spotted her in our front garden," Marcy explains, "looking a bit lost and confused. Do you think she's ill? Or maybe she's just getting a bit old and funny in the –"

"No, no, she's fine," I say, before Marcy

has a chance to put her foot in it. I put Queen Sardine down on the pavement and stroke her rain-slicked fur. "Thanks for bringing her back, though." I grin at Marcy then all of a sudden feel awkward. Did she get our letter? I hope she at least read it. "Er, soooo . . ." I say, feeling embarrassed. "Are you, er, feeling better? We missed you at school."

Marcy's mouth quirks up in a shy smile. "Yeah," she says. "I'll see you on Monday."

Yay! Then she *did* get the letter. And our 'sorry's must have worked!

Marcy's dad offers to drive us home, but I'm happy walking in the rain now that Sardine's back. He makes me take an umbrella so I don't get soaked, and Her Majesty stays close to keep dry.

I wave goodbye to Marcy and her dad, then start heading home with Sardine at my heels.

"You can thank me later," she says, looking up with a smug smile.

"Thank you for *what*, exactly?"

"For helping with Marcy, of course," she says as we

sidestep a puddle. "For bringing her to you, and getting you two talking again!"

My mouth falls open. That's what she was up to? Nope. There's more to it. She just doesn't want to admit it.

Mum opens the front door before we reach it.

"Oh, thank goodness! Get inside. It's raining cats and dogs!"

I close the umbrella and dash in. Mum hovers in the doorway waiting for Her Majesty, who is now looking up at the sky, confused, rain splattering her face.

"Well, Queen Sardine? In or out? Quick, quick!" hurries Mum.

Sardine gives the sky one last worried look, then she slowly slinks inside.

"She's stark raving nuts, your mum!" hiss-pers Her Royal Highness, and I have to laugh. I guess human sayings don't always make much sense to cats.

"Gosh, Ivy, you're soaked," says Mum, wringing out my t-shirt. "Go change into something dry. There's a pile of clean clothes on your bed."

I'm not really that wet. Or maybe I am. But I'm more interested in hearing what my feline friend's got to say for herself. So, once we're in my room, I sit down on the rug, ignoring my wet clothes, and I pull Sardine onto my lap.

"So that was the only reason you disappeared?" I ask. "To help me out?"

"Yes, of course," she says.

"Nothing to do with what happened last night then?"

"I don't know what you mean," she says, licking her already-damp fur.

I'm getting cross now. "You *do* know! You made up that stuff about Princess

Persia, and you said you'd fix it but you *haven't*. The Kipper Street cats have been accusing Princess Persia of all sorts. We looked everywhere for you this morning."

"All right, all right!" Queen Sardine groans, then she buries her face under her paws.

"I'm sorry," she mumbles. "I had to get away. Visiting Marcy was a spur of

the moment decision. I thought, why not do something *good* while I'm doing something cowardly? You don't understand, Ivy... I just couldn't bear to tell the other cats that I – I –"

"Lied?"

"Yes! Fine, I lied, okay?"

"Look," I say, "I *do* understand. I messed up with Marcy, didn't I? It's horrible feeling guilty and it's embarrassing saying sorry. But..."

"But I need to say it anyway. Yes, yes, I know. I see that now," she says. And, well, I've had some time to think, and I've had an idea. I'll make it better. Trust me."

Then I think she starts humming. (It's hard to be sure. I've never heard a cat hum before.)

"Prrrmmm... prrrrrmmmm..."

"Is that a tune, Your Majesty?" I ask.

"Hmm? What? Well of course it is. There has to be a tune... all part of the plan," she mutters, and starts humming again.

"So I'll tell the cats you're back, shall I? You know they're still out looking for you." *While you're in here making weird noises*, I think.

She stops prrrmmm-ing. Her head snaps up, and her eyes are wide.

"Oh. Yes, of course! They need to know their queen is safe but, Ivy..."

"Yes, Your Majesty?"

"Tell them I can't see them yet. Tell them I have important plans to attend to."

"Okay, but —"

"Promise!" she cries. "I can't see them. Not yet!"

"I promise!" I say, befuddled.

Geez. Talk about getting your whiskers in a tangle.

"Very well. Run along then," she says, flicking her paw towards the door. "Right away if you don't mind."

"Fine," I sigh, dragging my soggy

bottom off the floor. "But this plan had better be good."

"Good? This plan, Miss Ivy, is spectacular! Best plan ever," she says. However, instead of planning, she looks like she's settling down for a nap.

"Oh, and Ivy," she yawns, just as I'm heading off.

"Yes," I say. *What now?*

Queen Sardine stretches out, tummy up, looking at me with half-shut eyes.

"Thank you," she says sleepily. "For searching for me. You're sudge... a good ... fwend." She slurs her words as she slips off to sleep.

And even though I'm wet and tired, even though my best friend is bossy and bananas, even though I still need to face the Kipper Street cats... I smile.

SHOWTIME!

It's Monday morning registration, and I'm worried Marcy's changed her mind, that she's not coming to school after all. But then . . .

"Sorry I'm late, Mr Gubbins."

She waves a little 'hello' in my and Kei's direction, then joins us at the table.

Good. This is good. Now we can finally tell Marcy, face-to-face (or face-to-face-to-face because there's three of us), just how much we want to be mates again.

"Quiet!" says Mr Gubbins.

Drat. Mr G calls the register in silence. But as soon as he's done...

"Marcy, we just wanted to say —" whispers Kei.

"*Quiet!*" repeats Mr Gubbins. "All eyes on me. Today's the big day. Time to show the school your, erm... skills. Talents and what-not. Now, are there any last-minute changes I should know about? No?"

Marcy's hand flies up, then in a tiny voice she says, "Excuse me, Mr Gubbins, but..."

"Yes? What is it, Marcy? And why aren't you in your dance outfit like the other two?"

"I – I don't think I can dance today. I'm not ready. I've been ill . . . I'm still not feeling quite right..." she says. Then Marcy looks at us and whispers, "Is that okay?"

We nod. Of course it's okay. She must be really nervous being back at school and still not really knowing anyone.

"Right. Yes. Fine," continues Mr Gubbins. He looks at his watch. "Good

grief, we're late! Okay, take what you need, and line up at the door. No talking. We're on stage in twenty minutes!"

This stinks. Marcy's stuck at the front of the line, and we're right at the back. I notice her fiddling with something. It looks like a small plastic tub.

The shushing teachers and chattering kids pile into the assembly hall while our class waits alongside the stage. As soon as everyone's sitting down, Mr Gubbins gives us the thumbs up.

Let the show begin...

Josh does his introduction thingy, and then everyone takes turns performing. Soon, Josh says the terrifying words: "And now, Kei and Ivy are going to do a dance." We both stand up, trying not to look at the hundreds of faces turned towards us. As I climb over our cross-legged classmates, someone taps my ankle.

Marcy.

"Here! Take this," she says, offering up the pot of glitter sprinkles. Oh. Oh! Now I see. But...

"That's okay," I whisper, smiling. It's a nice thought, but I want to show Marcy that we listened to her ideas. She's right: real dancers don't need glitter.

We stand at the front of the stage, me and Kei. Mr Gubbins' finger hovers over the CD player, waiting for a nod from Kei that we're ready to begin. But Kei's got other ideas.

"Hello, er, everyone," she says. "We'll do the dance in a second. It's not very good, so don't get too excited."

The kids start murmuring and Mr

Gubbins pulls a frantic *what's-she-doing?* face at me.

I shrug. I've no idea what she's doing!

"But first off," says Kei, "we need to say sorry to someone." Kei looks at me, and I finally get it. This is our moment to really make things right.

"Y-yeah... Yes, that's right!" I stammer. I'm not so good at this talking-to-millions-of-people thing. "Marcy — that's Marcy over there," I say, pointing in her direction. "Well, she's a r-really dood

gancer... I mean, *good dancer*! And sh– she tried to help make our dance b–better, I mean..." My tongue is twisting all over the place and giggles are bubbling up from the audience. *Yikes!* "Anyway..." I look at Kei and she nods.

"We're sorry," we say, together.

We look over to Marcy and, thank-flipping-pancakes, she's smiling!

Then Kei yells, "Hit it!" and suddenly the music's playing and we're supposed to know what we're doing!

We shimmy back, spring forward, twirl left, twirl –

Ow! – right onto my knees... but I'm up – I'm fine, I'm fine... We stretch high, low, jump back, strike a pose. Now for the tricky-to-remember bit, oh crumbs!

The beat speeds up; faster, faster. We spin, roll forward, spring up, and...

"Umph!" I turn to see that somehow Kei's landed on the floor.

"Keep going, just keep going," she hisses at me, picking herself up.

But I've lost it now. What's next? The double-jump? The hip-jiggle? Jazz hands?

Kei shrugs, she doesn't know either. We're hopeless! Hopeless and helpless.

There's a rumble of chuckles from the audience, followed by a hiss of 'Shh!' from the teachers, but the kids are right. We look ridiculous, standing up here without a stinking clue what to do. My face is burning with embarrassment. Seriously, you could fry an egg on one of my cheeks and sizzle a sausage on the other.

Kei sighs, defeated. We're about to give up and ask Mr Gubbins to switch off the music, when...

"Come on, you can do it! Turn, shimmy, twist!" Marcy's on the stage with us, the glitter pot clasped in her fist. She's dancing with us, urging us on. And it's working! It's coming back to me... Yes, yes – we do know this!

From the corner of my eye, I see Kei grin. She's finding her feet again, getting back into the flow of the dance. With Marcy leading us, it almost feels like we know what we're doing. *Jump, lunge, turn ...* this isn't half bad!

Marcy really is flipping brilliant! She twirls and jumps and stretches and poses, and – best of all – we keep up. Yeah, we're not proper dancers like Marcy, but we're doing okay. We're doing all right!

As we approach the end of the song, the hard bit of our dance – the *probably-going-to-goof-it-up* bit – I chance a look at Kei. She has a determined glint in her eye, like a tiger. Like Queen Sardine when she's in fly-catching mode. And I try to feel the same. *Skip, balance, twist...*

Easy, I can do this.

Except, I can't! I can't do this. I'm stiffening up, too frightened to move. I'm going to ruin it, I'm going to . . .

"Come on, Ivy, follow me! Like we practised! One, two, three, *now*!" Marcy is a little way in front of me. She talks as we move, ignoring the audience. So I ignore them too, and find I *can* do it. I can!

We jump high, spin... and dip down into our finishing pose. As we do, the kids in the audience gasp. An actual, real, proper gasp!

Then the music fades. Marcy grins at me, grins at Kei, and she holds the glitter pot up high, twists the lid, and...

WHOOSH!

Diamond rain sparkles down on us, coating

the stage in rainbow glitter. And all I can hear are whoops and claps. I can't stop smiling.

"You two were right," Marcy whispers, "The glitter was the best bit." She winks at us as we leave the stage, and something fluffy and fuzzy and warm occurs to me. If things can turn out this brilliantly perfect for me and Marcy then maybe, just maybe, things will work out brilliantly purrrfect for Queen Sardine too!

THE KIPPER STREET CHORUS

As I walk home I can't help smiling. It's been a glitterific, sparkletastic day. Everyone wants to be Marcy's friend, now that they've seen her dancing. She's like a school celebrity!

KIPPER STREET

I see Queen Sardine waiting for me as I turn onto Kipper Street. She's wearing her fishbone crown, which means something important is happening.

"It's time I told the other cats about my little... *fib*, Miss Ivy. I'm meeting them in front of Princess Persia's house any minute now. I thought maybe you might come with me?"

She sounds like she doesn't really mind either way, but I know that deep down she wants me there, just in case it goes badly.

I rush home, say hi to Mum and beg her to let me play out, then I run back to Persia's house, where the Kipper Street cats are gathered.

They've formed a little crowd on the pavement, all of them bowed low and facing Queen Sardine.

I look over the fence to see if Persia's in her garden, but no, she's inside the

house, peeking through the window.

"Arise, citizens! No bowing," says Queen Sardine, her mouth set in a grim line. "I... I have a confession to make."

Silence.

Her Majesty coughs, shuffles on the spot, then dips her head, letting the crown roll gently onto the pavement.

The cats all *MEOWL* in horror!

"Your Majesty!" says Benny. "What is it? What's wrong?"

"I lied to you!" she shouts. Sardine's been hiding the truth all this time, and now it's bursting out. "Princess Persia didn't say any of those cruel things about you, or say that she was better than the Kipper Street cats. I made it up. All of it!"

The cats back up, bristling and confused.

"I was scared," Sardine explains. "Scared that you'd like her more than me. Scared you'd want *her* to be your queen."

She hangs her head, nudging the fishbone crown with her nose. "And I thought she wanted... Never mind. Anyway, it was all lies. She's just like the rest of us, not snooty at all. Princess Persia is new to our neighbourhood, and we

134

need to show her how Kipper Street cats treat newcomers."

"Do we pee on their doorsteps?" asks Sprout.

"No, we don't, Sprout," she sighs. "We purr at them. We welcome them."

I wonder if Princess Persia can hear through the glass. Yes, I think she can. Her ears are twitching and her eyes are thin slits as she secretly watches.

The cats murmur and mew among themselves for a moment, then little Sprout steps forward. "So she didn't say any of those things? She didn't call us riff- raff?"

Queen Sardine shakes her head, staring at the pavement.

"I'm sorry," she sighs, stooping to nudge the crown with her nose. "Maybe *she* should be your —"

"WAIT!"

We all turn, just as Princess Persia jumps through an open window. "No, Your Majesty!" she shouts. "It's a brave, *brave* cat who can admit she's wrong and say she's sorry!"

"Very brave," mutter the others, nodding their heads in agreement.

"And I wasn't exactly blameless," continues Persia. "I did wind you up a *teeny* bit on purpose. I'm sorry, Your Majesty. You're clearly kinder than I first thought."

Queen Sardine grins at me, and I grin back at her. Though she seems to be forgetting something. *Say sorry back*, I think. *Say sorry back!*

"You're forgiven," sighs Sardine, and all the cats cheer.

Phew! Queen Sardine really can do nothing wrong as far as these cats are concerned. They love her, and that's that!

Princess Persia stoops, carefully picks the crown up in her mouth, and places it back on Queen Sardine.

"Long live the queen!" she calls, and the cats echo it back:

"Long live the queen!"

Their cheers turn into noisy mews and happy purrs, and we all jump when Sardine suddenly yells, "Silence! ... *please.*"

"Ahem," she coughs, squirming a little. "Princess Persia, I owe you an apology..."

"No, no that's quite all right," says Persia, but Sardine just keeps on talking.

"So, I'd like to sing you something. I know you like opera, so I've written one just for you. I wanted to to show you how truly sorry I am."

This was her plan? This is what all the bizarre humming has been about?

She turns to the others and mumbles, "I'll sing it a few times, join in when you've learned the words!"

And then Queen Sardine begins to sing her song:

Persia, oh Persia,
I truly am sorry,
I've been such a terrible fool.
I got rather jealous and nervous and so...
I did something wickedly cruel!

The rumours I spread
Were so easily said,
But my brain wasn't really engaged.

I didn't expect them to spread as they did
Causing anger and horror and rage...

So Persia, oh Persia,
Forgive me I beg you!
I'll do all I can to amend.
And maybe, who knows,
If you give me a chance,
You might learn to call me a friend.

And before long, all the cats are joining in: Persia, oh Persia...

... and it goes on and on, and round and round, until I can't help joining in too!

"Again! Again!" Persia cries with a Cheshire-cat grin, just as we're coming to the end for the fourth time. And so we start over from the beginning! We sing our hearts out, loud and pretty much tunelessly, but meaning every word. And we're so wrapped up in singing that no one sees Princess Persia's front door slowly easing open.

When I finally notice a man and a woman standing there, mouths wide, my cheeks flush hot and I freeze. Persia's people! Oh, good grief...

This must look crazy. I should go, run! I'm just about to dash off home, when...

"Amazing!" announces the woman. "Please, keep going. Keep going! Peter, this is incredible," she says to the man. "Quick! Fetch my camera."

Oh. Well, yes – I guess it is pretty incredible. And, yes, I probably look like a crazy person, but... it's fun! And it's super important to Sardine, so who cares if I look like a ninny?

The man, Peter, comes back with the woman's camera, and it's the hugest camera I've ever seen.

"Keep singing, I'm filming everything," the woman says. "We're journalists. This'll make a great story! I can see the headline now: *Girl Leads Cat Choir!* This is phenomenal..."

My cheeks are blazing but I keep singing. It feels like years before we reach the end of the song, and when we do I have to smile.

Because, once Queen Sardine has sung her last wobbly note, she leans forward and rubs faces with Princess Persia. If people did that it'd be weird, but for cats, well, it just shows that they're friends. Which is pretty flipping brilliant, I reckon.

The other cats mewl and purr, and when the cats start wandering off, I pick up Queen Sardine.

"Well done, Your Majesty," I whisper.

"Oh, Ivy," she tuts. "It was nothing!" But we both know that's not true.

I turn to Persia's people and nod 'goodbye' – they're still filming, but I think it's time Sardine and I made our way home.

As I carry her up the garden path to

our front door, I cuddle her tight.

"We did well today, you and me," I tell her. "It's not easy saying sorry. But we did it anyway."

And I can't help grinning.

"How will we celebrate?" she asks me.

I laugh. I can feel her tummy rumbling, and I know she'll be wanting some fish when we get inside.

"Cod, tuna or pilchards, Your Majesty?"

She nuzzles her face into my neck, and sighs a happy sigh. "You're so good to me, Ivy," she says with a purr.

I know exactly what she's after.

"All three, then?" I ask and, if it's possible, her purr gets even louder.

"Cod, tuna, pilchards . . . purrrrrrrr… All fishy three!"

And with that, my best friend and I have a very scaly, very stinky, very happy ending.

GIRL LEADS

Young Squiddly resident achieves the impossible!

IVY MEADOWS, 8, has been training local cats to sing, with miraculous results.

Miss Meadow's cat choir was discovered serenading a new feline resident, no doubt trying to initiate her into the singing troupe. It is thought that Ivy's ability

CAT CHOIR

to mimic cat sounds by singing perfectly out of tune, has in some way 'hit a chord' with the animals.

Young Ivy's neighbours had been unaware of her cat-taming skills until we brought video evidence to their attention. Surprisingly, many took the news in their stride. "Oh yes, that's Ivy, all right! She's always been so wonderful with our Sardeeny-weeny-kins," said local resident Mrs Trott, and Mrs Dodd commented, "Ivy always talks to them cats so nicely. It's no wonder they listen to her."

One can only wonder what's next for Ivy and her caterwauling choir. Whatever happens, it's bound to be fan-tabby-tastic.

Find out how Ivy first
met Queen Sardine…

...and don't miss Ivy and
Queen Sardine's next adventure.

QUEEN
SARDINE
in Kitten Chaos

COMING SOON!